HORRID
HENRY'S
UNDERPANTS

Francesca Simon
Illustrated by Tony Ross

Orion
Children's Books

First published in Great Britain in 2003
by Orion Children's Books
Reissued in paperback 2008
by Orion Children's Books
a division of the Orion Publishing Group Ltd
Orion House
5 Upper Saint Martin's Lane
London WC2H 9EA
An Hachette Livre UK Company

6

Text © Francesca Simon 2003
Illustrations © Tony Ross 2003

The moral right of Francesca Simon and Tony Ross
to be identified as author and illustrator
of this work has been asserted.

The Orion Publishing Group's policy is to use papers that are natural,
renewable and recyclable products and made from wood grown in
sustainable forests. The logging and manufacturing processes are expected to
conform to the environmental regulations of the country of origin.

A catalogue record for this book is available from the British Library.

Printed in Great Britain by Clays Ltd, St Ives plc

www.horridhenry.co.uk
www.orionbooks.co.uk

HORRID HENRY's UNDERPANTS

Francesca Simon spent her childhood on the beach
in California, and then went to Yale and Oxford
Universities to study medieval history and literature.
She now lives in London with her family. She has
written over 45 books and won the Children's Book
of the Year in 2008 at the Galaxy British Book Awards
for *Horrid Henry and the Abominable Snowman*.

Also by Francesca Simon

Don't Cook Cinderella
Helping Hercules

and for younger readers
Don't Be Horrid, Henry

The Topsy-Turvies
Illustrated by Emily Bolam

There is a complete list of **Horrid Henry** titles
at the end of the book.
Horrid Henry is also available on audio CD and
digital download, all read by Miranda Richardson.

Visit Horrid Henry's website at
www.horridhenry.co.uk for competitions,
games, downloads and a monthly newsletter

For Gina Kovarsky

CONTENTS

1

HORRID HENRY
EATS A VEGETABLE

"Ugggh! Gross! Yuck! Bleeeeeech!"

Horrid Henry glared at the horrible,
disgusting food slithering on his plate.
Globby slobby blobs. Bumpy lumps.
Rubbery blubbery globules of glop.
Ugghh!

How Dad and Mum and Peter could
eat this swill without throwing up was
amazing. Henry poked at the white,
knobbly clump. It looked like brains. It
felt like brains. Maybe it was . . .
Ewwwwwwww.

Horrid Henry pushed away his plate.

"I can't eat this," moaned Henry. "I'll
be sick!"

"Henry! Cauliflower cheese is delicious," said Mum.

"And nutritious," said Dad.

"I love it," said Perfect Peter. "Can I have seconds?"

"It's nice to know *someone* appreciates my cooking," said Dad. He frowned at Henry.

"But I hate vegetables," said Henry. Yuck. Vegetables were so . . . healthy. And tasted so . . . vegetably. "I want pizza!"

"Well, you can't have it," said Dad.

"Ralph has pizza and chips every night at *his* house," said Henry. "And Graham *never* has to eat vegetables."

"I don't care what Ralph and Graham eat," said Mum.

"You've got to eat more vegetables," said Dad.

"I eat loads of vegetables," said Henry.

"Name one," said Dad.

"Crisps," said Henry.

"Crisps aren't vegetables, are they, Mum?" said Perfect Peter.

"No," said Mum. "Go on, Henry."

"Ketchup," said Henry.

"Ketchup is not a vegetable," said Dad.

"It's impossible cooking for you," said Mum.

"You're such a picky eater," said Dad.

"I eat loads of things," said Henry.

"Like what?" said Dad.

"Chips. Crisps. Burgers. Pizza. Chocolate. Sweets. Cake. Biscuits. Loads of food," said Horrid Henry.

"That's not very healthy, Henry," said Perfect Peter. "You haven't said any fruit or vegetables."

"So?" said Henry. "Mind your own business, Toad."

"Henry called me Toad," wailed Peter.

"Ribbet. Ribbet," croaked Horrid Henry.

"Don't be horrid, Henry," snapped Dad.

"You can't go on eating so unhealthily," said Mum.

"Agreed," said Dad.

Uh oh, thought Henry. Here it comes. Nag nag nag. If there were prizes for best naggers Mum and Dad would win every time.

"I'll make a deal with you, Henry," said Mum.

"What?" said Henry suspiciously. Mum and Dad's "deals" usually involved his doing something horrible, for a pathetic reward. Well no way was he falling for that again.

"If you eat all your vegetables for five nights in a row, we'll take you to Gobble and Go."

Henry's heart missed a beat. Gobble and Go! Gobble and Go! Only Henry's favourite restaurant in the whole wide world. Their motto: "The chips just keep on coming!" shone forth from a purple neon sign. Music blared from twenty loudspeakers. Each table had its own TV. You could watch the chefs heat up your food in a giant microwave. Best of all, grown-ups never wanted to hang about for hours and chat. You ordered, gobbled, and left. Heaven.

And what fantastic food! Jumbo burgers. Huge pizzas. Lakes of ketchup. As many chips as you could eat. Fifty-two different ice creams. And not a vegetable in sight.

For some reason Mum and Dad hated Gobble and Go. They'd taken him once, and sworn they would never go again.

And now, unbelievably, Mum was offering.

"Deal!" shouted Henry, in case she changed her mind.

"So we're agreed," said Mum. "You eat your vegetables every night for five nights, and then we'll go."

"Sure. Whatever," said Horrid Henry eagerly. He'd agree to anything for a meal at Gobble and Go. He'd agree to dance naked down the street singing "Hallelujah! I'm a nudie!" for the chance to eat at Gobble and Go.

Perfect Peter stopped eating his cauliflower. He didn't look very happy.

"I always eat *my* vegetables," said Peter. "What's my reward?"

"Health," said Mum.

Day 1. String beans.

"Mum, Henry hasn't eaten any beans yet," said Peter.

"I have too," lied Henry.

"No you haven't," said Peter. "I've been watching."

"Shut up, Peter," said Henry.

"Mum!" wailed Peter. "Henry told me to shut up."

"Don't tell your brother to shut up," said Mum.

"It's rude," said Dad. "Now eat your veg."

Horrid Henry glared at his plate, teeming with slimy string beans. Just like a bunch of green worms, he thought. Yuck.

He must have been
mad agreeing to eat
vegetables for five
nights in a row.
He'd be poisoned
before day three.
Then they'd be sorry.
"How could we have been so
cruel?" Mum would shriek. "We've killed
our own son," Dad would moan. "Why
oh why did we make him eat his
greens?" they would sob.

Too bad he'd be dead so he couldn't
scream, "I told you so!"

"We have a deal, Henry," said Dad.

"I know," snapped Henry.

He cut off the teeniest, tiniest bit of
string bean he could.

"Go on," said Mum.

Slowly, Horrid Henry lifted his fork
and put the poison in his mouth.

Aaaarrrgggghhhhhh! What a horrible

taste! Henry spat and spluttered as the sickening sliver of string bean stuck in his throat.

"Water!" he gasped.

Perfect Peter speared several beans and popped them in his mouth.

"Great string beans, Dad," said Peter. "So crispy and crunchy."

"Have mine if you like them so much," muttered Henry.

"I want to see you eat every one of those string beans," said Dad. "Or no Gobble and Go."

Horrid Henry scowled. No way was he eating another mouthful. The taste was too horrible. But, oh, Gobble and Go. Those burgers! Those chips! Those TVs!

There had to be another way. Surely he, King Henry the Horrible, could defeat a plate of greens?

Horrid Henry worked out his battle

plan. It was dangerous. It was risky. But what choice did he have?

First, he had to distract the enemy.

"You know, Mum," said Henry, pretending to chew, "you were right. These beans *are* very tasty."

Mum beamed.

Dad beamed.

"I told you you'd like them if you tried them," said Mum.

Henry pretended to swallow, then speared another bean. He pushed it round his plate.

Mum got up to refill the water jug. Dad turned to speak to her. Now was his chance!

11

Horrid Henry stretched out his foot under the table and lightly tickled Peter's leg.

"Look out, Peter, there's a spider on your leg."

"Where?" squealed Peter, looking frantically under the table.

Leap! Plop!

Henry's beans hopped onto Peter's plate.

Peter raised his head.

"I don't see any spider," said Peter.

"I knocked it off," mumbled Henry, pretending to chew vigorously.

Then Peter saw his plate, piled high with string beans.

"Ooh," said Peter, "lucky me! I thought I'd finished!"

Tee hee, thought Horrid Henry.

Day 2. Broccoli.

Plip!

A piece of Henry's broccoli "accidentally" fell on the floor. Henry kicked it under Peter's chair.

Plop! Another piece of Henry's broccoli fell. And another. And another.

Plip plop. Plip plop. Plip plop.

Soon the floor under Peter's chair was littered with broccoli bits.

"Mum!" said Henry. "Peter's making a mess."

"Don't be a telltale, Henry," said Dad.

"He's always telling on *me*," said Henry.

Dad checked under Peter's chair.

"Peter! Eat more carefully. You're not a baby any more."

Ha ha ha thought Horrid Henry.

Day 3. Peas.

Squish!

Henry flattened a pea under his knife.

Squash!

Henry flattened another one.

Squish. Squash.

Squish. Squash.

Soon every pea was safely squished and hidden under Henry's knife.

"Great dinner, Dad," said Horrid Henry. "Especially the peas. I'll clear," he added, carrying his plate to the sink and quickly rinsing his knife.

Dad beamed.

"Eating vegetables is making you helpful," said Dad.

"Yes," said Henry sweetly. "It's great being helpful."

Day 4. Cabbage.

Buzz.

Buzz.

"A fly landed on my cabbage!" shrieked Henry. He swatted the air with his hands.

"Where?" said Mum.

"There!" said Henry. He leapt out of his seat. "Now it's on the fridge!"

"Buzz," said Henry under his breath.

"I don't see any fly," said Dad.

"Up there!" said Henry, pointing to the ceiling.

Mum looked up.

Dad looked up.

Peter looked up.

Henry dumped a handful of cabbage in the bin. Then he sat back down at the table.

"Rats," said Henry. "I can't eat the rest of my cabbage now, can I? Not after a filthy horrible disgusting fly has walked all over it, spreading germs and dirt and poo and—"

"All right all right," said Dad. "Leave the rest."

I am a genius, thought Horrid Henry, smirking. Only one more battle until - Vegetable Victory!

Day 5. Sprouts.

Mum ate her sprouts.

Dad ate his sprouts.

Peter ate his sprouts.

Henry glared at his sprouts. Of all the miserable, rotten vegetables ever invented, sprouts were the worst. So bitter. So stomach-churning. So . . . green.

But how to get rid of them? There was Peter's head, a tempting target. A very tempting target. Henry's sprout-flicking fingers itched. No, thought Horrid Henry. I can't blow it when I'm so close.

Should he throw them on the floor? Spit them in his napkin?

Or – Horrid Henry beamed.

There was a little drawer in the table in front of Henry's chair. A perfect, brussels sprout-sized drawer.

Henry eased it open. What could be simpler than stuffing a sprout or two inside while pretending to eat?

17

Soon the drawer was full. Henry's plate was empty.

"Look Mum! Look Dad!" screeched Henry. "All gone!" Which was true, he thought gleefully.

"Well done, Henry," said Dad.

"Well done, Henry," said Peter.

"We'll take you to Gobble and Go tomorrow," said Mum.

"Yippee!" screamed Horrid Henry.

Mum, Dad, Henry, and Peter walked up the street.

Mum, Dad, Henry, and Peter walked down the street.

Where was Gobble and Go, with its flashing neon sign, blaring music, and purple walls? They must have walked past it.

But how? Horrid Henry looked about wildly. It was impossible to miss Gobble and Go. You could see that neon sign for miles.

"It was right here," said Horrid Henry.
But Gobble and Go was gone.
A new restaurant squatted in its place.
"The Virtuous Veggie," read the sign.
"The all new, vegetable restaurant!"

Horrid Henry gazed in horror at the menu posted outside.

Cabbage Casserole
Pop-up Peas
Spinach Surprise
Sprouts a go-go
Choice of rhubarb or
broccoli ice cream

"Yummy!" said Perfect Peter.
"Look, Henry," said Mum. "It's serving all your new favourite vegetables."

Horrid Henry opened his mouth to protest. Then he closed it. He knew when he was beaten.

2

HORRID HENRY'S UNDERPANTS

A late birthday present! Whoopee! Just when you thought you'd got all your loot, more treasure arrives.

Horrid Henry shook the small thin package. It was light. Very light. Maybe it was — oh, please let it be — MONEY! Of course it was money. What else could it be? There was so much stuff he needed: a Mutant Max lunchbox, a Rapper Zapper Blaster, and, of course, the new Terminator Gladiator game he kept seeing advertised on TV. Mum and Dad were so mean and horrible, they wouldn't buy it for him. But he could buy whatever he liked with his own

money. So there. Ha ha ha ha ha.
Wouldn't Ralph be green with envy
when he swaggered into school with a
Mutant Max lunchbox? And no way
would he even let Peter touch his
Rapper Zapper Blaster.

So how much money had he been
sent? Maybe enough for him to buy
everything! Horrid Henry tore off the
wrapping paper.

AAAAARRRRGGGHHHHH!
Great-Aunt Greta had done it again.

Great-Aunt Greta thought he was a
girl. Great-Aunt Greta had been told ten
billion times that his name was Henry,
not Henrietta, and that he wasn't four
years old. But every year Peter would get
£10, or a football, or a computer game,
and he would get a Walkie-Talkie-Teasy-
Weasy-Burpy-Slurpy Doll. Or a Princess
Pamper Parlour. Or Baby Poopie Pants.
And now this.

Horrid Henry picked up the birthday card. Maybe there was money inside. He opened it.

Dear Henny,
You must be such a big girl now, so I know you'd love a pair of big girl pants. I'll bet pink is your favourite colour.
Love, Great-Aunt Greta

Horrid Henry stared in horror at the frilly pink lacy knickers, decorated with glittery hearts and bows. This was the worst present he had ever received. Worse than socks. Worse than handkerchiefs. Even worse than a book.

Bleeech! Ick! Yuck! Horrid Henry chucked the hideous underpants in the bin where they belonged.

Ding dong.

Oh no! Rude Ralph was here to play. If he saw those knickers Henry would never hear the end of it. His name would be mud forever.

Clump clump clump.

Ralph was stomping up the stairs to his bedroom. Henry snatched the terrible pants from the bin and looked around his room wildly for a hiding place. Under the pillow? What if they had a pillow fight? Under the bed? What if they played hide and seek? Quickly Henry stuffed them in the back of his pants drawer. I'll get rid of them the moment Ralph leaves, he thought.

"Mercy, Your Majesty, mercy!"

King Henry the Horrible looked down at his snivelling brother.

"Off with his head!" he ordered.

"Henry! Henry! Henry!" cheered his grateful subjects.

"HENRY!"

King Henry the Horrible woke up. His Medusa mother was looming above him.

"You've overslept!" shrieked Mum. "School starts in five minutes! Get dressed! Quick! Quick!" She pulled the duvet off Henry.

"Wha—wha?" mumbled Henry.

Dad raced into the room.

"Hurry!" shouted Dad. "We're late!" He yanked Henry out of bed.

25

Henry stumbled around his dark bedroom. Half-asleep, he reached inside his underwear drawer, grabbed a pair, then picked up some clothes off the floor and flung everything on. Then he, Dad, and Peter ran all the way to school.

"Margaret! Stop pulling Susan's hair!"

"Ralph! Sit down!"

"Linda! Sit up!"

"Henry! Pay attention!" barked Miss Battle-Axe. "I am about to explain long division. I will only explain it once. You take a great big number, like 374, and then divide it—"

Horrid Henry was not paying attention. He was tired. He was crabby. And for some reason his pants were itchy.

These pants feel horrible, he thought. And so tight. What's wrong with them?

Horrid Henry sneaked a peek.

And then Horrid Henry saw what

pants he had on. Not
his Driller Cannibal
pants. Not his
Marvin the Maniac
ones either. Not
even his old Gross-
Out ones, with the
holes and the droopy
elastic.

He, Horrid Henry, was wearing frilly
pink lacy girls' pants covered in glittery
hearts and bows. He'd completely forgotten
he'd stuffed them into his pants drawer last
month so Ralph wouldn't see them. And
now, oh horror of horrors, he was wearing
them.

Maybe it's a nightmare, thought
Horrid Henry hopefully. He pinched his
arm. Ouch! Then, just to be sure, he
pinched William.

"Waaaaah!" wailed Weepy William.

"Stop weeping, William!" said Miss

Battle-Axe. "Now, what number do I need—"

It was not a nightmare. He was still in school, still wearing pink pants.

What to do, what to do?

Don't panic, thought Horrid Henry. He took a deep breath. Don't panic. After all, no one will know. His trousers weren't see-through or anything.

Wait. What trousers was he wearing? Were there any holes in them? Quickly Horrid Henry twisted round to check his bottom.

Phew. There were no holes. What luck he hadn't put on his old jeans with the big rip but a new pair.

He was safe.

"Henry! What's the answer?" said Miss Battle-Axe.

"Pants," said Horrid Henry before he could stop himself.

The class burst out laughing.

"Pants!" screeched Rude Ralph.

"Pants!" screeched Dizzy Dave.

"Henry. Stand up," ordered Miss Battle-Axe.

Henry stood. His heart was pounding. Slip!

Aaaarrrghhh! The lacy ruffle of his pink pants was showing! His new trousers were too big. Mum always bought him clothes that were way too big so he'd grow into them. These were the falling-down ones he'd tried on yesterday. Henry gripped his trousers tight and yanked them up.

29

"What did you say?" said Miss Battle-Axe slowly.

"Ants," said Horrid Henry.

"Ants?" said Miss Battle-Axe.

"Yeah," said Henry quickly. "I was just thinking about how many ants you could divide by — by that number you said," he added.

Miss Battle-Axe glared at him.

"I've got my eye on you, Henry," she snapped. "Now sit down and pay attention."

Henry sat. All he had to do was tuck in his T-shirt. That would keep his trousers up. He'd look stupid but for once Henry didn't care.

Just so long as no one ever knew about his pink lacy pants.

And then Henry's blood turned to ice. What was the latest craze on the playground? De-bagging. Who'd started it? Horrid Henry. Yesterday he'd chased Dizzy

Dave and pulled down his trousers. The
day before he'd done the same thing to
Rude Ralph. Just this morning he'd de-
bagged Tough Toby on the way into class.

They'd all be trying to de-bag him now.

I have to get another pair of pants,
thought Henry desperately.

Miss Battle-Axe passed round the
maths worksheets. Quickly Horrid Henry
scribbled down: 3, 7, 41, 174, without
reading any questions. He didn't have
time for long division.

31

Where could he find some other pants? He could pretend to be sick and get sent home from school. But he'd already tried that twice this week. Wait. Wait. He was brilliant. He was a genius. What about the Lost and Found? Someone, some time, must have lost some pants.

DING! DING!

Before the playtime bell had finished ringing Horrid Henry was out of his seat and racing down the hall, holding tight to his trousers. He checked carefully to make sure no one was watching, then ducked into the Lost and Found. He'd hide here until he found some pants.

The Lost and Found was stuffed with clothes. He rummaged through the mountains of lost shoes, socks, jackets, trousers, shirts, coats, lunchboxes, hats, and gloves. I'm amazed anyone leaves school wearing *anything*, thought Horrid

Henry, tossing another sweatshirt over his shoulder.

Then – hurray! Pants. A pair of blue pants. What a wonderful sight.

Horrid Henry pulled the pants from the pile. Oh no. They were the teeniest, tiniest pair he'd ever seen. Some toddler must have lost them.

Rats, thought Horrid Henry. Well, no way was he wearing his horrible pink pants a second longer. He'd just have to trade pants with someone. And Horrid Henry had the perfect someone in mind.

Henry found Peter in the playground playing tag with Tidy Ted.

"I need to talk to you in private," said Henry. "It's urgent."

"What about?" said Peter cautiously.

"It's top secret," said Henry. Out of the corner of his eye he saw Dave and Toby sneaking towards him.

Top secret! Henry never shared top secret secrets with Peter.

"Quick!" yelped Henry. "There's no time to lose!"

He ducked into the boys' toilet. Peter followed.

"Peter, I'm worried about you," said Horrid Henry. He tried to look concerned.

"I'm fine," said Peter.

"No you're not," said Henry. "I've heard bad things about you."

"What bad things?" said Peter anxiously. Not — not that he had run across the carpet in class?

"Embarrassing rumours," said Horrid Henry. "But if I don't tell you, who will? After all," he said, putting his arm around Peter's shoulder, "it's my job to look after you. Big brothers should look out for little ones."

Perfect Peter could not believe his ears.

"Oh, Henry," said Peter. "I've always wanted a brother who looked after me."

"That's me," said Henry. "Now listen. I've heard you wear baby pants."

"I do not," said Peter. "Look!" And he

showed Henry his Daffy and her Dancing Daisies pants.

Horrid Henry's heart went cold. Daffy and her Dancing Daisies! Ugh. Yuck. Gross. But even Daffy would be a million billion times better than pink pants with lace ruffles.

"Daffy Daisy are the most babyish pants you could wear," said Henry. "Worse than wearing a nappy. Everyone will tease you."

Peter's lip trembled. He hated being teased.

"What can I do?" he asked.

Henry pretended to think. "Look. I'll do you a big favour. I'll swap my pants for yours. That way *I'll* get teased, not you."

"Thank you, Henry," said Peter. "You're the best brother in the world." Then he stopped.

"Wait a minute," he said suspiciously, "let's see your pants."

"Why?" said Henry.

"Because," said Peter, "how do I know you've even got pants to swap?"

Horrid Henry was outraged.

"Of course I've got pants," said Henry.

"Then show me," said Peter.

Horrid Henry was trapped.

"OK," he said, giving Peter a quick flash of pink lace.

Perfect Peter stared at Henry's underpants.

"Those are your pants?" he said.

"Sure," said Horrid Henry. "These are big boy pants."

37

"But they're pink," said Peter.

"All big boys wear pink," said Henry.

"But they have lace on them," said Peter.

"All big boys' pants have lace," said Henry.

"But they have hearts and bows," said Peter.

"Of course they do, they're big boy pants," said Horrid Henry. "You wouldn't know because you only wear baby pants."

Peter hesitated.

"But . . . but . . . they look like — girls' pants," said Peter.

Henry snorted. "Girls' pants! Do you think *I'd* ever wear girls' pants? These are what all the big kids are wearing. You'll be the coolest kid in class in these."

Perfect Peter backed away.

"No I won't," said Peter.

"Yes you will," said Henry.

"I don't want to wear your smelly pants," said Peter.

"They're not smelly," said Henry. "They're brand new. Now give me your pants."

"NO!" screamed Peter.

"YES!" screamed Henry. "Give me your pants!"

"What's going on in here?" came a voice of steel. It was the Head, Mrs Oddbod.

"Nothing," said Henry.

"There's no hanging about the toilets at playtime," said Mrs Oddbod. "Out of here, both of you."

Peter ran out the door.

Now what do I do, thought Horrid Henry.

Henry ducked into a stall and hid the pink pants on the ledge above the third toilet. No way was he putting those pants back on. Better Henry no pants than Henry pink pants.

★

At lunchtime Horrid Henry dodged
Graham. He dodged Toby by the
climbing frame. During last play Dave
almost caught him by the water
fountain but Henry was too quick.
Ralph chased him into class but Henry
got to his seat just in time. He'd done
it! Only forty-five minutes to go until
home time. There'd be no de-bagging
after school with parents around.
Henry couldn't believe it. He was safe
at last.

He stuck out his tongue at Ralph.

"Nah nah ne nah ne," he jeered.

Miss Battle-Axe clapped her claws.

"Time to change for P.E.," said Miss
Battle-Axe.

P.E.! It couldn't be – not a P.E. day.

"And I don't care if aliens stole your
P.E. kit, Henry," said Miss Battle-Axe,
glaring at him. "No excuses."

That's what she thought. He had the

perfect excuse. Even a teacher as mean
and horrible as Miss Battle-Axe would
not force a boy to do P.E. without pants.

Horrid Henry went up to Miss Battle-
Axe and whispered in her ear.

"Forgot your pants, eh?" barked
Miss Battle-Axe loudly.

Henry blushed
scarlet. When
he was king
he'd make
Miss Battle-
Axe walk
around town every
day wearing pants on her head.

"Well, Henry, today is your lucky
day," said Miss Battle-Axe, pulling
something pink and lacy out of her
pocket. "I found these in the boys'
toilets."

"Take them away!" screamed Horrid
Henry.

3

HORRID HENRY'S SICK DAY

Cough! Cough!

Sneeze! Sneeze!

"Are you all right, Peter?" asked Mum.

Peter coughed, choked, and spluttered.

"I'm OK," he gasped.

"Are you sure?" said Dad. "You don't look very well."

"It's nothing," said Perfect Peter, coughing.

Mum felt Peter's sweaty brow.

"You've got a temperature," said Mum. "I think you'd better stay home from school today."

"But I don't want to miss school," said Peter.

"Go back to bed,"
said Mum.

"But I want to go
to school," wailed
Peter. "I'm sure I'll
be—" Peter's pale,
sweaty face turned green.
He dashed up the stairs to the loo. Mum
ran after him.

Bleeeeeeecchhhh. The horrible sound
of vomiting filled the house.

Horrid Henry stopped eating his toast.
Peter, stay at home? Peter, miss school?
Peter, laze about watching TV while he,
Henry, had to suffer a long hard day with
Miss Battle-Axe?

No way! He was
sick, too. Hadn't
he coughed twice
this morning?
And he had
definitely sneezed

44

last night. Now that he thought about it, he could feel those flu germs invading. Yup, there they were, marching down his throat.

Stomp stomp stomp marched the germs. Mercy! shrieked his throat. Ha ha ha gloated the germs.

Horrid Henry thought about those spelling words he hadn't learnt. The map he hadn't finished colouring. The book report he hadn't done.

Oww. His throat hurt.

Oooh. His tummy hurt.

Eeek. His head hurt.

Yippee! He was sick!

So what would it be?

Maths or Mutant Max?

Reading or relaxing?

Commas or comics?

Tests or TV?

Hmmm, thought Horrid Henry. Hard choice.

Cough. Cough.

Dad continued reading the paper.

COUGH! COUGH! COUGH! COUGH! COUGH!

"Are you all right, Henry?" asked Dad, without looking up.

"No!" gasped Henry. "I'm sick, too. I can't go to school."

Slowly Dad put down his newspaper.

"You don't look ill, Henry," said Dad.

"But I am," whimpered Horrid Henry. He clutched his throat. "My throat really hurts," he moaned. Then he added a few coughs, just in case.

"I feel weak," he groaned. "Everything aches."

Dad sighed.

"All right, you can stay home," he said.

Yes! thought Horrid Henry. He was amazed. It usually took much more moaning and groaning before his mean, horrible parents decided he was sick enough to miss a day of school.

"But no playing on the computer," said Dad. "If you're sick, you have to lie down."

Horrid Henry was outraged.

"But it makes me feel better to play on the computer," he protested.

"If you're well enough to play on the computer, you're well enough to go to school," said Dad.

Rats.

Oh well, thought Horrid Henry. He'd get his duvet, lie on the sofa and watch loads of TV instead. Then Mum would

bring him cold drinks, lunch on a tray, maybe even ice cream. It was always such a waste when you were too sick to enjoy being sick, thought Horrid Henry happily.

He could hear Mum and Dad arguing upstairs.

"I need to go to work," said Mum.

"I need to go to work," said Dad.

"I stayed home last time," said Mum.

"No you didn't, I did," said Dad.

"Are you sure?" said Mum.

"Yes," said Dad.

"Are you sure you're sure?" said Mum.

Horrid Henry could hardly believe his ears. Imagine arguing over who got to stay home! When he was grown-up he was going to stay home full time, testing computer games for a million pounds a week.

He bounced into the sitting room. Then he stopped bouncing. A horrible, ugly, snotty creature was stretched out

under a duvet in the comfy black chair.
Horrid Henry glanced at the TV.
A dreadful assortment of wobbling
creatures were dancing and prancing.

TRA LA LA LA LA,
WE LIVE AT NELLIE'S
WE'VE ALL GOT BIG BELLIES
WE EAT PURPLE JELLIES
AT NELLIE'S NURSERY (tee hee)

Horrid Henry sat down on the sofa.

"I want to watch *Robot Rebels*," said
Henry.

"I'm watching *Nellie's Nursery*," said
Peter, sniffing.

"Stop sniffing," said Henry.

"I can't help it, my nose is running,"
said Peter.

"I'm sicker than you, and *I'm* not
sniffing," said Henry.

"I'm sicker than you," said Peter.

"Faker."

"Faker."

"Liar."

"Liar!"

"MUM!" shrieked Henry and Peter.

Mum came into the room, carrying a tray of cold drinks and two thermometers.

"Henry's being mean to me!" whined Peter.

"Peter's being mean to *me*!" whined Henry.

"If you're well enough to fight, you're well enough to go to school, Henry," said Mum, glaring at him.

"I wasn't fighting, Peter was," said Henry.

"Henry was," said Peter, coughing.

Henry coughed louder.

Peter groaned.

Henry groaned louder.

"Uggghhhhh," moaned Peter.

"Uggghhhhhhhhh," moaned Henry. "It's not fair. I want to watch *Robot Rebels*."

"I want to watch *Nellie's Nursery*," whimpered Peter.

"Peter will choose what to watch because he's the sickest," said Mum.

Peter, sicker than he was? As if. Well, no way was Henry's sick day going to be ruined by his horrible brother.

"I'm the sickest, Mum," protested Henry. "I just don't complain so much."

Mum looked tired. She popped one thermometer into Henry's mouth and the other into Peter's.

51

"I'll be back in five minutes to check them," she said. "And I don't want to hear another peep from either of you," she added, leaving the room.

Horrid Henry lay back weakly on the sofa with the thermometer in his mouth. He felt terrible. He touched his forehead. He was burning! His temperature must be 105!

I bet my temperature is so high the thermometer won't even have enough numbers, thought Henry. Just wait till Mum saw how ill he was. Then she'd be sorry she'd been so mean.

Perfect Peter started groaning. "I'm going to be sick," he gasped, taking the thermometer from his mouth and running from the room.

The moment Peter left, Henry leapt up from the sofa and checked Peter's thermometer. 101 degrees! Oh no, Peter had a temperature. Now Peter would start getting *all* the attention. Mum would make Henry fetch and carry for him. Peter might even get extra ice cream.

Something had to be done.

Quickly Henry plunged Peter's thermometer into the glass of iced water.

Beep. Beep. Horrid Henry took out his own thermometer. It read 98.6F. Normal.

Normal! His temperature was normal? That was impossible. How could his temperature be normal when he was so ill?

If Mum saw that normal temperature she'd have him dressed for school in three seconds. Obviously there was something wrong with that stupid thermometer.

Horrid Henry held it to the light bulb. Just to warm it up a little, he thought.

Clump. Clump.

Yikes! Mum was coming back.

Quickly Henry yanked Peter's thermometer out of the iced water and replaced his own in his mouth. Oww! It was hot.

"Let's see if you have a temperature," said Mum. She took the thermometer out of Henry's mouth.

"127 degrees!" she shrieked.

Oops.

"The thermometer must be broken," mumbled Henry. "But I still have a temperature. I'm boiling."

"Hmmn," said Mum, feeling Henry's forehead.

Peter came back into the sitting room slowly. His face was ashen.

"Check *my* temperature, Mum," said

Peter. He lay back weakly on the pillows.

Mum checked Peter's thermometer.

"57 degrees!" she shrieked.

Oops, thought Horrid Henry.

"That one must be broken too," said Henry.

He decided to change the subject fast.

"Mum, could you open the curtains please?" said Henry.

"But I want them closed," said Peter.

"Open!"

"Closed!"

"We'll leave them closed," said Mum.

Peter sneezed.

"Mum!" wailed Henry. "Peter got snot all over me."

"Mum!" wailed Peter. "Henry's smelly."

Horrid Henry glared at Peter.

Perfect Peter glared at Henry.

Henry whistled.

Peter hummed.

"Henry's whistling!"

"Peter's humming!"

"MUM!" they screamed. "Make him stop!"

"That's enough!" shouted Mum. "Go to your bedrooms, both of you!"

Henry and Peter heaved their heavy bones upstairs to their rooms.

"It's all your fault," said Henry.

"It's yours," said Peter.

The front door opened. Dad came in. He looked pale.

"I'm not feeling well," said Dad. "I'm going to bed."

Horrid Henry was bored. Horrid Henry was fed up. What was the point of being sick if you couldn't watch TV and you couldn't play on the computer?

"I'm hungry!" complained Horrid Henry.

"I'm thirsty," complained Perfect Peter.

"I'm achy," complained Dad.

"My bed's too hot!" moaned Horrid Henry.

"My bed's too cold," moaned Perfect Peter.

"My bed's too hot and too cold," moaned Dad.

Mum ran up the stairs.

Mum ran down the stairs.

"Ice cream!" shouted Horrid Henry.

"Hot water bottle!" shouted Perfect Peter.

"More pillows!" shouted Dad.

Mum walked up the stairs.

Mum walked down the stairs.

"Toast!" shouted Henry.

"Tissues!" croaked Peter.

"Tea!" gasped Dad.

"Can you wait a minute?" said Mum. "I need to sit down."

"NO!" shouted Henry, Peter, and Dad.

"All right," said Mum.

She plodded up the stairs.

She plodded down the stairs.

"My head is hurting!"

"My throat is hurting!"

"My stomach is hurting!"

Mum trudged up the stairs.

Mum trudged down the stairs.

"Crisps," screeched Henry.

"Throat lozenge," croaked Peter.

"Hankie," wheezed Dad.

Mum staggered up the stairs.

Mum staggered down the stairs.

Then Horrid Henry saw the time. Three-thirty. School was finished! The weekend was here! It was amazing, thought Horrid Henry, how much better he suddenly felt.

Horrid Henry threw off his duvet and leapt out of bed.

"Mum!" he shouted. "I'm feeling much better. Can I go and play on the computer now?"

Mum staggered into his room.

"Thank goodness you're better, Henry," she whispered. "I feel terrible. I'm going to bed. Could you bring me a cup of tea?"

What?

"I'm busy," snapped Henry.

Mum glared at him.

"All right," said Henry, grudgingly. Why couldn't Mum get her own tea? She had legs, didn't she?

Horrid Henry escaped into the sitting room. He sat down at the computer and loaded "Intergalactic Robot Rebellion: This Time It's Personal". Bliss. He'd zap some robots, then have a go at "Snake Master's Revenge".

"Henry!" gasped Mum. "Where's my tea?"

"Henry!" rasped Dad. "Bring me a drink of water!"

"Henry!" whimpered Peter. "Bring me an extra blanket."

Horrid Henry scowled. Honestly, how was he meant to concentrate with all these interruptions?

"Tea!"

"Water!"

"Blanket!"

"Get it yourself!" he howled. What was he, a servant?

"Henry!" spluttered Dad. "Come up here this minute."

Slowly, Horrid Henry got to his feet. He looked longingly at the flashing screen. But what choice did he have?

"I'm sick too!" shrieked Horrid Henry. "I'm going back to bed."

4

HORRID HENRY'S THANK YOU LETTER

Ahh! This was the life! A sofa, a telly, a bag of crisps. Horrid Henry sighed happily.

"Henry!" shouted Mum from the kitchen. "Are you watching TV?"

Henry blocked his ears. Nothing was going to interrupt his new favourite TV programme, *Terminator Gladiator*.

"Answer me, Henry!" shouted Mum. "Have you written your Christmas thank you letters?"

"NO!" bellowed Henry.

"Why not?" screamed Mum.

"Because I haven't," said Henry. "I'm busy." Couldn't she leave him alone for two seconds?

Mum marched into the room and switched off the TV.

"Hey!" said Henry. "I'm watching *Terminator Gladiator*."

"Too bad," said Mum. "I told you, no TV until you've written your thank you letters."

"It's not fair!" wailed Henry.

"I've written all *my* thank you letters," said Perfect Peter.

"Well done, Peter," said Mum. "Thank goodness *one* of my children has good manners."

Peter smiled modestly. "I always write mine the moment I unwrap a present. I'm a good boy, aren't I?"

"The best," said Mum.

"Oh, shut up, Peter," snarled Henry.

"Mum! Henry told me to shut up!" said Peter.

"Stop being horrid, Henry. You will

write to Aunt Ruby, Great-Aunt Greta and Grandma now."

"Now?" moaned Henry. "Can't I do it later?"

"When's later?" said Dad.

"Later!" said Henry. Why wouldn't they stop nagging him about those stupid letters?

Horrid Henry hated writing thank you letters. Why should he waste his precious time saying thank you for presents? Time he could be spending reading comics, or watching TV. But no. He would barely unwrap a present before Mum started nagging. She even expected him to write to Great-Aunt Greta and thank her for the Baby Poopie Pants doll. Great Aunt-Greta for one did not deserve a thank you letter.

This year Aunt Ruby had sent him a hideous lime green cardigan.

Why should he thank her for that? True, Grandma had given him £15, which was great. But then Mum had to spoil it by making him write her a letter too. Henry hated writing letters for nice presents every bit as much as he hated writing them for horrible ones.

"You have to write thank you letters," said Dad.

"But why?" said Henry.

"Because it's polite," said Dad.

"Because people have spent time and money on you," said Mum.

So what? thought Horrid Henry. Grown-ups had loads of time to do whatever they wanted. No one told them, stop watching TV and write a thank you letter. Oh no. They could do it whenever they felt like it. Or not even do it at all.

And adults had tons of money compared to him. Why shouldn't they spend it buying him presents?

"All you have to do is write one page," said Dad. "What's the big deal?"

Henry stared at him. Did Dad have no idea how long it would take him to write one whole page? Hours and hours and hours.

"You're the meanest, most horrible parents in the world and I hate you!" shrieked Horrid Henry.

"Go to your room, Henry!" shouted Dad.

"And don't come down until you've written those letters," shouted Mum. "I am sick and tired of arguing about this."

Horrid Henry stomped upstairs.

Well, no way was he writing any thank you letters. He'd rather starve. He'd rather die. He'd stay in his room for a month. A year. One day Mum and Dad would come up to check on him and all they'd find would be a few bones. Then they'd be sorry.

Actually, knowing them, they'd probably just moan about the mess. And then Peter would be all happy because he'd get Henry's room and Henry's room was bigger.

Well, no way would he give them the satisfaction. All right, thought Horrid Henry. Dad said to write one page. Henry would write one page. In his biggest, most gigantic handwriting, Henry wrote:

Dear Aunt Ruby,
Thank you
for the
present.
Henry

That certainly filled a whole page, thought Horrid Henry.

Mum came into the room.

"Have you written your letters yet?"

"Yes," lied Henry.

Mum glanced over his shoulder.

"Henry!" said Mum. "That is not a proper thank you letter."

"Yes it is," snarled Henry. "Dad said to write one page so I wrote one page."

"Write five sentences," said Mum.

Five sentences? Five whole sentences? It was completely impossible for anyone to write so much. His hand would fall off.

"That's way too much," wailed Henry.

"No TV until you write your letters," said Mum, leaving the room.

Horrid Henry stuck out his tongue. He had the meanest, most horrible parents in the world. When he was king any parent who even whispered the words "thank you letter" would get fed to the crocodiles.

They wanted five sentences? He'd give them five sentences. Henry picked up his pencil and scrawled:

Dear Aunt Ruby,
No thank you for the horrible present. It is the worst present I have ever had.
Anyway, didn't some old Roman say it was better to give than to receive? So in fact, you should be writing me a thank you letter.
Henry
P.S. Next time just send money.

There! Five whole sentences. Perfect, thought Horrid Henry. Mum said he had to write a five sentence thank you letter. She never said it had to be a *nice* thank you letter. Suddenly Henry felt quite cheerful. He folded the letter and popped it in the stamped envelope Mum had given him.

One down. Two to go.

In fact, Aunt Ruby's no thank you letter would do just fine for Great-Aunt Greta. He'd just substitute Great-Aunt Greta's name for Aunt Ruby's and copy the rest.

Bingo. Another letter was done.

Now, Grandma. She *had* sent money so he'd have to write something nice.

"Thank you for the money, blah blah blah, best present I've ever received, blah blah blah, next year send more money, £15 isn't very much, Ralph got £20 from *his* grandma, blah blah blah."

What a waste, thought Horrid Henry as he signed it and put it in the envelope, to spend so much time on a letter, only to have to write the same old thing all over again next year.

And then suddenly Horrid Henry had a wonderful, spectacular idea. Why had he never thought of this before? He would be rich, rich, rich. "There goes money-bags Henry," kids would whisper enviously, as he swaggered down the street followed by Peter lugging a hundred videos for Henry to watch in his mansion on one of his twenty-eight giant TVs. Mum and Dad and Peter would be living in their hovel somewhere, and if they were very, very nice to him Henry *might* let them watch one of his smaller TVs for fifteen minutes or so once a month.

Henry was going to start a business. A business guaranteed to make him rich.

"Step right up, step right up," said Horrid Henry. He was wearing a sign saying: HENRY'S THANK YOU LETTERS: "Personal letters written just for you." A small crowd of children gathered round him.

"I'll write all your thank you letters for you," said Henry. "All you have to do

is to give me a stamped, addressed envelope and tell me what present you got. I'll do the rest."

"How much for a thank you letter?" asked Kung-Fu Kate.

"£1," said Henry.

"No way," said Greedy Graham.

"99p," said Henry.

"Forget it," said Lazy Linda.

"OK, 50p," said Henry. "And two for 75p."

"Done," said Linda.

Henry opened his notebook. "And what were the presents?" he asked. Linda made a face. "Handkerchiefs," she spat. "And a bookmark."

"I can do a 'no thank you' letter," said Henry. "I'm very good at those."

Linda considered.

"Tempting," she said, "but then mean Uncle John won't send something better next time."

Business was brisk. Dave bought three. Ralph bought four "no thank you's". Even Moody Margaret bought one. Whoopee, thought Horrid Henry. His pockets were jingle-jangling with cash. Now all he had to do was to write seventeen letters. Henry tried not to think about that.

The moment he got home from school Henry went straight to his room. Right, to work, thought Henry. His heart sank as he looked at the blank pages. All those letters! He would be here for weeks. Why had he ever set up a letter-writing business?

But then Horrid Henry thought. True, he'd promised a personal letter but how would Linda's aunt ever find out that Margaret's granny had received the same one? She wouldn't! If he used the computer, it would be a cinch. And it would be a letter sent personally,

thought Henry, because I am a
person and I will personally print it
out and send it. All he'd have to do
was to write the names at the top and
to sign them. Easy-peasy lemon
squeezy.

Then again, all that signing. And
writing all those names at the top.
And separating the thank you letters
from the no thank you ones.

Maybe there was a better way.

Horrid Henry sat down at the
computer and typed:

Dear Sir or Madam,

That should cover everyone, thought
Henry, and I won't have to write anyone's
name.

Thank you /No thank you/ for the
a) wonderful

77

b) horrible

c) disgusting

present. I really loved it/hated it. In fact, it is the best present/worst present/I have ever received. I /played with it/ broke it/ ate it/spent it/ threw it in the bin/ straight away. Next time just send lots of money.

Best wishes/ worst wishes/

Now, how to sign it? Aha, thought Henry.

Your friend or relative.

Perfect, thought Horrid Henry. Sir or Madam knows whether they deserve a thank you or a no thank you letter. Let them do some work for a change and tick the correct answers.

Print.

Print.

Print.

Out spewed seventeen letters. It only took a moment to stuff them in the envelopes. He'd pop the letters in the postbox on the way to school.

Had an easier way to become a millionaire ever been invented, thought Horrid Henry, as he turned on the telly?

Ding dong.

It was two weeks after Henry set up "Henry's Thank You Letters."

Horrid Henry opened the door.

A group of Henry's customers stood there, waving pieces of paper and shouting.

"My granny sent the letter back and now I can't watch TV for a week," wailed Moody Margaret.

"I'm grounded!" screamed Aerobic Al.

"I have to go swimming!" screamed Lazy Linda.

"No sweets!" yelped Greedy Graham.

"No pocket money!" screamed Rude
Ralph.

"And it's all your fault!" they
shouted.

Horrid Henry glared at his angry
customers. He was outraged. After
all his hard work, *this* was the thanks
he got?

"Too bad!" said Horrid Henry as he
slammed the door. Honestly, there was
no pleasing some people.

"Henry," said Mum. "I just had the strangest phone call from Aunt Ruby . . ."

HORRID HENRY BOOKS

Horrid Henry
Horrid Henry and the Secret Club
Horrid Henry Tricks the Tooth Fairy
Horrid Henry's Nits
Horrid Henry Gets Rich Quick
Horrid Henry's Haunted House
Horrid Henry and the Mummy's Curse
Horrid Henry's Revenge
Horrid Henry and the Bogey Babysitter
Horrid Henry's Stinkbomb
Horrid Henry's Underpants
Horrid Henry Meets the Queen
Horrid Henry and the Mega-Mean Time Machine
Horrid Henry and the Football Fiend
Horrid Henry's Christmas Cracker
Horrid Henry and the Abominable Snowman
Horrid Henry Robs the Bank

Colour books

Horrid Henry's Big Bad Book
Horrid Henry's Wicked Ways
Horrid Henry's Evil Enemies
Horrid Henry Rules the World

Joke Books

Horrid Henry's Joke Book
Horrid Henry's Jolly Joke Book
Horrid Henry's Mighty Joke Book

Activity Books

Horrid Henry's Brainbusters
Horrid Henry's Headscratchers
Horrid Henry's Mindbenders
Horrid Henry's Colouring Book
Horrid Henry's Puzzle Book
Horrid Henry's Sticker Book
Horrid Henry's Crazy Crosswords
Horrid Henry's Mad Mazes
Horrid Henry's Wicked Wordsearches

Horrid Henry is also available on audio CD and digital download, all read by Miranda Richardson.

"A hoot from beginning to end ... As always, Miranda Richardson's delivery is perfection and the manic music is a delight."
Daily Express

"Long may this dreadful boy continue to terrorise all who know him. He's a nightmare, but so entertaining . . . Miranda Richardson's spirited reading is accompanied by a brilliant music soundtrack – they make a noisy and fun-filled duo."
Parents' Guide

HORRID HENRY

Henry is dragged to dancing class against his will; vies with Moody Margaret to make the yuckiest Glop, goes camping in France and tries to be good like Perfect Peter – but not for long.

HORRID HENRY
AND THE SECRET CLUB

Horrid Henry gets an injection, torments his little brother Perfect Peter, creates havoc at his own birthday party, and plans sweet revenge when Moody Margaret won't let him into her Secret Club.

HORRID HENRY
TRICKS THE TOOTH FAIRY

(Originally published as
Horrid Henry and the Tooth Fairy)
Horrid Henry tries to trick the
Tooth Fairy into giving him more
money, sends Moody Margaret packing,
causes his teachers to run screaming
from school, and single-handedly
wrecks a wedding.

HORRID HENRY'S
NITS

Scratch. Scratch. Scratch. Horrid Henry
has nits – and he's on a mission to give
them to everyone else too. After that, he
can turn his attention to wrecking the
school trip, ruining his parents' dinner
party, and terrifying Perfect Peter.

HORRID HENRY'S
HAUNTED HOUSE

Horrid Henry slugs it out with
Perfect Peter over the remote control,
stays in a haunted house and gets a nasty
shock, discovers where X marks the spot
in the hidden treasure competition
and stars on TV.

HORRID HENRY
GETS RICH QUICK

(Originally published as
Horrid Henry Strikes It Rich)
Horrid Henry tries to sell off Perfect
Peter and get rich, makes sure he gets
the presents he wants for Christmas,
sabotages Sports Day at school and
runs away from home.